WITHDRAWN

Curious George®
Lemonade Stand

Adaptation by Erica Zappy Wainer
Based on the TV series teleplay "Curious George
Makes a Stand" written by Gentry Menzel

Houghton Mifflin Harcourt
Boston New York

For information about permission to reproduce selections from this book, write to trade.permissions@hmhco.com <mailto:trade.permissions@hmhco.com> or to permissions, Houghton Mifflin Harcourt Publishing Company, 3 Park Av 19th Floor, New York, New York 10016.

ISBN: 978-0-544-65221-7 paper-over-board
ISBN: 978-0-544-65223-1 paperback

Design by Afsoon Razavi
Art adaptation by Rudy Obrero and Kaci Obrero

www.hmhco.com
Printed in Malaysia
TWP 10 9 8 7 6 5 4 3 2
4500589949

AGES	GRADES	GUIDED READING LEVEL	READING RECOVERY LEVEL	LEXILE ® LEVEL
4-7	1	J	17	410L

George loved playing soccer.
But he needed a new ball.

"When I was young, I got a new soccer ball by running a lemonade stand," the man with the yellow hat said.

This gave George an idea.
There was a lot of lemonade in the
refrigerator.

The man with the yellow hat was going out.
"We can have some lemonade together
when I get home, George!" he said.

George looked at the lemonade in the refrigerator.
He really wanted a new soccer ball.

George brought the lemonade outside.
He borrowed a lemon crate from the
shopkeeper down the street.
The crate would make a perfect stand.

George set up his lemonade stand
outside his apartment and waited.

Out came the doorman. He was hot.
"Hey, is that lemonade?" he asked.
George handed him a full carton of
lemonade.

"That's too much, George! Do you have any cups?" the doorman asked. George ran inside. He came back with cups and filled one up to the top. "I still can't drink all of that, George!" the doorman said.

The doorman poured half the lemonade
into another cup. "That's better," he said.
George didn't know you could make one
cup of lemonade into two cups!

The doorman gave George a quarter
for the lemonade.
A quarter? George was confused.
Where was the soccer ball?

George waited and waited, but there were no more customers. He needed a better spot for his stand. But where?

Soon George saw Betsy.
"I can help you sell lemonade," Betsy
said.

Sell? Now George understood. He needed to *earn* the money to *buy* a soccer ball.

Betsy had seen a construction site nearby.
The workers were tired and thirsty.
It would be a great spot to sell lemonade.

It didn't take long for the workers to line up!
Everyone loved George's lemonade.
His stand was a success.

Soon George was
down to his last two cups of lemonade.
But there were still four thirsty workers
in line!
George remembered the doorman's
trick.
He split the two cups in
half to make four!

Now George had enough money
to buy a soccer ball. George and
Betsy went straight to the toy store
to buy one.

Then George remembered his friend.
The man was looking forward to a glass
of lemonade, but George had sold it all.
George had one more big idea.

George used
his money to buy more lemonade.
But his friend had a big idea too!
He brought home a new soccer ball
for George. George was a very happy
monkey.

Make Your Own Lemonade

With a few simple ingredients, you can make your own lemonade at home! Enjoy it on a warm day, or set up your own lemonade stand to save up for something special.

You will need:
5-6 lemons
6 cups of water
1 cup of sugar
a measuring cup
a pitcher
a long spoon
ice

Ask a grownup to help you cut the lemons in half. Squeeze juice out of five or six fresh lemons. When you have filled a one-cup measuring cup, pour the juice into a pitcher filled with six cups of water. Add a cup of sugar (or a little less) to sweeten it. Stir the water, lemon juice, and sugar together with a long spoon until it is all mixed together. Add ice or put in the refrigerator to chill. Then enjoy!

Finding Fractions

Running a lemonade stand taught George about dividing and making different portions. When the doorman gets too much lemonade, he shows George how to divide one serving in half to make two servings. When you divide something in half, you create two equal parts.
You can also divide a whole into thirds (three equal parts), fourths (four equal parts), and so on. Halves, thirds, and fourths are called fractions.

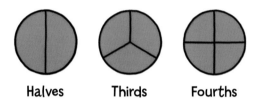

Halves   Thirds   Fourths

You can find fractions all around you!

Have a grownup help you find fractions around your house. Look for objects at home that are divided into parts, like closet doors, window panes, and couch cushions. Make a list of the objects you find and how many parts each one is divided into. What did you find that was divided into the most equal parts?

If you're looking for more fractions, you can always make your own! Dividing into fractions is a great way to share!

31901060163377